Girl & Flame

A Novella

Melissa Reddish

Praise for Melissa Reddish's
My Father is an Angry Storm Cloud

"Reddish populates her stories with miniature men, bus-driving ghosts, and babies growing in gardens. But she also populates them with parents, children, and lovers, all struggling to find connection. *My Father is an Angry Storm Cloud* reminds us it's hardest to love the ones we hold closest." —**Christy Crutchfield, author of *How to Catch a Coyote***

"*My Father is an Angry Storm Cloud* takes aimless characters from the mundane world of suburbs and dead-end jobs and places them in situations where saviors can quickly become enemies, imaginary friends go on rampages and feral children will literally eat your house. Melissa Reddish is a brilliant storyteller who plays off our own fears of irrelevance and gives us something extraordinary to hold on to." —**Jonathan Harper, author of *Daydreamers***

"These stories are coming for you. Some are deliberate shadows and others are monster babies, but either way you will agree that with this collection of Hawthorne-inflected tales Melissa Reddish claims a place as one of our most exciting American fabulists, alongside Kelly Link, Matt Bell, and Karen Russell." —**Laura Ellen Scott, author of *The Juliet* and *Death Wishing***

Praise for Melissa Reddish's
Girl & Flame

"A blowtorch of modern death and rebirth, *Girl & Flame* tries to contain 'the girl who burned her father, brother, lover' and the animistic fire that snaps and pops within. Reddish has forged an incendiary and highly readable hybrid prose. Keep the fire extinguisher handy." —**Mel Bosworth, co-author of *Camouflage Country* & author *Freight***

"Short sharp fragments of flame build an entire world that is hard to look away from. Reddish's prose dazzles and burns. It's a fire that's impossible to ignore. *Girl & Flame* reverberates with danger and foreboding, masked in an expert language that only Reddish can harness." —**Sarah Rose Etter, author of *Tongue Party***

"Melissa Reddish's latest tour de force, *Girl & Flame*, is a haunting flash novella/verse-narrative that blends magical realism and psychological drama into a startling love story about madness that is, at turns, both crude and courtly." —**Laura Ellen Scott, author of *The Juliet* and *Death Wishing***

Girl & Flame

A Novella

Melissa Reddish

Conium Press
Portland, OR

Girl & Flame: A Novella
by Melissa Reddish

Published in the United States of America
Conium Press
Portland, Oregon
http://www.coniumreview.com

© 2016 Melissa Reddish & Conium Press

ISBN-10 1-942387-08-3
ISBN-13 978-1-942387-08-4
Library of Congress Control Number: 2016941405

Cover Typeface: "Helvetidoodle," by Edward Townend
Cover Image: © Wavebreak Media Micro / Dollar Photo Club
Cover Design & Interior Layout: James R. Gapinski

Excerpts of this novella have been previously published in *Iron Horse Literary Review* and *The Conium Review Online Compendium*.

Contents

I. The Girl

1. After the Fire

The smoke was tremendous—choking flesh made sky. It was even lovelier than the flames, great hands wrenching wood from stone, not a surgeon's hands—anatomical, precise—but a drunk old pugilist ready to go down swinging. Or maybe they were more like teeth, ripping and tearing in one long devouring breath the entirety of my childhood. Of course, it wasn't just the house. My father, brother, lover all burned. The three men in my life, their bodies grown round with beer and steak and wine. My mother had disappeared long ago. Hers was a diminishment, a gradual acknowledgment that her space grew smaller and smaller with each breath of my father or brother or lover, until finally, one warm July morning, she exhaled and collapsed into memory. Now, the heat and smoke rise and take the shape of her, phoenix-like, though I know it is only an illusion, a trick of the mind to render what is painful, to feel the pleasure of lapping at old wounds. As my mother became air, my father, brother, and lover remain grounded, their bodies a kind of permanence. Now they are piles of ash and teeth and bone, ready to drift into a plate of spaghetti, to slip through the gears of a pocket watch, to be sucked into my little cousin's nose right before he sneezes.

2. The Ember That Follows Me

I didn't notice it at first, tiny incorporeal thing, lingering after the fire took everything. It hovers, tendril-bright, just above my head. It could be a piece of foundation or a bit of not-so-flame-retardant curtain, burning with the quiet intensity of sight. It has nowhere and nothing else to be. I hold out my hand and it lands, dust-mote of flame, and slowly begins burning through my skin. I place a washcloth beneath it. It takes an entire day to burn through the cloth. After all , isn't that what washcloths are for: to stave off entropy? In this way we travel, the ember and I, through the neighborhoods that once belonged to me, or perhaps, that belonged only to the slow rust-vine slipping around the playground like a noose. Ownership is tricky that way. When the filet of salmon slides through your stomach, does it remember the fisherman's daughter, the way she tucked her hair behind her ears when she was embarrassed? Does it remember last month's unseasonably warm rains? Does it remember Christ, the way He ripped it from one into many and then nothing? Does it think this tearing of flesh brings it closer to God?

3. The First Place We Travel

The ember seems to desire somewhere noisy and full of life. Perhaps its hunger is stronger than I realize; perhaps I mistake wisdom for patience. I am not interested in buildings filled with people who scrape their teeth against the sky, so we walk through the woods at the edge of town. The trees shake their mystery into the damp air. They don't seem to enjoy our presence. I remember the first time I kissed my now-dead lover underneath a sycamore covered in ants. That tree was dead, but my lover was still alive. The forest can tell I'm the kind of girl who ignores the pain of others. *Have you always been so selfish*, the tall pine in front of me asks. The ember comes to my defense with a stirring rendition of breakfast cereal. The trees shake their leaves at us, then their branches, then pour sap from several strategically placed holes. It is obscene. I lead the ember through the thick dead heart of the woods until we come to a cabin. It is made of logs but is not a log cabin. The chimney is not pouring smoke but it will soon. Inside there is a wooden bed and a wooden chest and a wooden rug and two wooden chairs. On the walls are wooden heads: bear, deer, elk. Their mouths are open and they are full of wooden teeth. *Good one*, I say to the trees. The trees shake with a mirth entirely at our expense. They are real assholes.

4. What Follows Us

We leave the forest and the cabin made of logs, but we aren't alone. A beast made of smoke and shadow crouches in the corner of our vision, waiting for us to turn our heads. I turn my head left, then right, and then slowly in a circle, but I cannot see him. The ember draws close and singes my hair. I rip my shirt and tie it in a knot to give the ember someplace to hide. Perhaps I too can find a wrinkle in the world to slip into, a place to stop and breathe. But the sun has flattened the afternoon, so there is nowhere else to go. My only choice is to keep walking, always with the humid breath of the beast at my back. When I run, he runs. When I walk, he walks. And when I finally lay down to sleep and dream, he does so as well. In my dream, he is a small black dog with eyes tightly shut. In his dream, I am a girl who killed everyone she loved: father, brother, lover. I struck the match and in my eyes, it gleamed. *I am coming for you*, I say to the beast. The beast wakes up panting and covered in sweat. How can he escape the girl with fire in her eyes? She is always looking for him, and if she ever catches him, she will hold him down with fingers like gunpowder, and he will burn.

5. The Second Place We Travel

I decide it's time for the ember to get a little air. It is looking a little limp, a sickly brownish-gold. No, not it. She. So we walk to the top of the Empire State Building. There are many people but also there is no one. I wonder how many will jump. Perhaps they will not throw their bodies but their sense of parental optimism or their tolerance for passive-aggressive comments from Cindy, who gave up gluten last winter and will not shut the hell up about it. Already they are shedding their sense of individuality in order to engage in a roof-wide narrative about the impermanence of the American Dream. Mostly it is based on *Dukes of Hazzard* and *You're Got Mail*. The ember flits from person to person, breathing in the smell of perfume and flammable fabrics. She surges, growing larger, heady from such unfettered kindling. Nobody seems to notice, which is for the best. No reason to panic at the top of the Empire State Building. There will be plenty of time for that loose feeling of dread after scaling such a grand structure and finding yourself wholly, irrevocably unchanged.

6. The Time that Can Pass After a Tragedy When Everyone Gets Sick of Your Whining

A couple weeks after the fire, the ember asks when I'm going to get a job. I hadn't really given it much thought. Before the fire that consumed everything I loved, I had worked as a mailroom clerk at a company that specialized in customizable office supplies. I placed all the envelopes into larger envelopes and sent them upstairs. The only person who ever bothered to learn my name was Nancy, the self-appointed keeper of birthdays. Every day Nancy ran from cubicle to cubicle getting everyone to sign a card. It was always someone's birthday in that vast building of customizable office supplies. My lover said that I was working below my means and I should return to school to study a trade like Nursing or Coquetry. But I always thought if I wasn't sorting mail, I would work on an Alaskan fishing boat and pull up net after net of cod, halibut, and flounder. If I stayed on the boat long enough, I would pull up a mermaid with scaly breasts and a whipping tail. She would stick her tongue in my mouth and it would taste of salt and lies. She would whisper in my ear the secrets of the ocean. She wouldn't do the same for any of the other fisherman whose desires were covered in brine. The ember is not amused by any of these anecdotes, but then again, I have never known fire to be especially subtle in either humor or passion.

7. A Partial List of Things Lost in the Fire

Taking out the trash; taking out the recycling; rolling the trash to the curb on Sunday night; the leaking dishwasher; the water spots on the glasses; the mismatched pull chains on the bedroom fan; all the burned-out light bulbs; all the used paper towels; all the socks with holes in them; the four broken glasses and the tiny shards of leftover glass beneath the fridge; the empty ice-cube tray that no one remembered to fill; the hum-dinga-ding of the dryer when it was finished; the broken front step; the broken back step; the fallen branches from last night's storm; the leaves in the gutter; the leaves on the lawn; the leaf inexplicably in my bed; *The Land Before Time* on video cassette; my mother's gold wedding ring; the dusty blinds; the family photos leading up the staircase; my father's favorite coffee mug; the broom in the hall closet; the bottles of Clorox, Bam!, and Windex, mostly full; the twenty-eight pairs of shoes; the thirty-one pairs of pants; the eighteen neckties; the single pair of cufflinks, never worn; the upstairs hamper (for shirts, pants, and other outerwear); the downstairs hamper (for underwear, socks, and towels); the set of Nutcracker decorations passed down from my grandmother; the set of nice cloth placemats for company; the dress I wore to Junior prom; my mother's jewelry box; my brother's stack of *Maxims*; the chipped clay pot from middle school used to collect coins; the box of extra cords nobody properly understood but kept out of a misguided sense of propriety; the alarm clock; the blue and yellow and pink sheets from each bed; what was on the sheets from each bed; the answering machine asking you to leave a message after the—

8. So I Get a Job

After several days of the ember flaming larger and larger, consuming all of the surrounding oxygen in not-so-silent protest, I finally agree to get a job. Since I do not have what you could call marketable skills, unless you count a vague sense (a kind of posterior tingling) when someone is giving a performance incongruent with their true sense of self, I settle on another office job. The building specializing in customizable office supplies is now a building specializing in customizable pet accessories, so I don't even have to apply. I'm taken upstairs to the seventh floor and led into a small, windowless room with a large conference table and three sets of metal filing cabinets. On the conference table are piles of documents. The man who led me upstairs, my direct supervisor or a reasonable facsimile, motions toward the documents with a thick white hand. I imagine biting that hand and coating my tongue with wax. His entire body seems to glow, but maybe it is just the A/C, which has been broken since Tuesday. He instructs me to sort all of the piles by weight. I pick up the first pile as he adjusts his glasses. *They all are the same*, I say. He nods like I finally understood. *Finish these by noon.* I consider the possibility that he doesn't mean physical weight but instead the weight of significance. Unfortunately, the documents are written in a set of undecipherable scribbles, so I'm unable to sort them by their relevance to the vast world of customizable pet supplies or by their ability to stir the emotions of an aloof and emotionally unavailable Japanese businessman. Finally, I sort the papers not by their physical weight or their intent, but instead by the primary color palate I imagine each document would embody when it was performed as a Broadway play. That works for a while, but then the palettes become too nuanced. (I mean, can anyone really tell the difference between salmon and coral?) The last few piles I sort by their feelings toward traditional romance; it turns out most of the documents are closet Meg Ryan fans, but only late at night when that guy they were casually IMing fails to write them back. (And, I mean, in that instance, who isn't?) At noon, my maybe-supervisor returns and shoves all of the piles into an oversized briefcase. *Take an extended lunch*, he tells me with a grin like fractured headlights. *You deserve it.*

9. What Happens in the After of Ever After

The next step after getting a job, the ember informs me, is finding a place to live. We have been sleeping in piles of dead leaves for several months, so it's time to find a place to call our own. The first apartment I find is covered in a mother's thin-lipped disappointment, so I search until I find one at the outskirts of town that is the site of a gruesome murder. I like the idea of a place with history. The apartment has four rooms: kitchen, living room, bathroom, and bedroom. The ember probably doesn't need an entire room of her own, I figure, what with her being a tiny mote of flame and all. After we move our stuff and then our bodies into the space, the ember asks if I want to return to the site of the fire to see if I can rescue any mementos—photos or knickknacks or perhaps a support beam. I tell her there's no point: our memories are pooling into stardust, and soon they will explode. She wants to know where she fits into the narrative of the all-consuming fire, and I tell her the truth: she is a product of the unfulfilled desires of the house. She pouts in the corner of the kitchen for a while, spending an alarming amount of time near the oven, but eventually she comes around, flaming low near my refurbished mattress. I accept her heat as apology and salve, and I spend the rest of the night with her in the quickening dusk, imagining future

Christmas carols at our front door and then setting the carolers quietly aflame, both of us curled into a life poured into hearty mugs, generous and filling, if not perfectly measured.

10. The Man Who Knocks on our Door

After a long afternoon of twisting our faces into different shapes, we hear a knock on our door. On the other side is an old man with long gray hair and a short gray moustache and a long gray beard. His eyes hold the image of a beckoning finger and the sound of wind on a mountaintop. He holds up a photograph of a girl, her hair long and blonde and perfectly combed, her clothing covered in bees. We invite him in and he eats all of the macaroni and cheese we had been saving for the holidays. We give him a fork and he throws it into the ceiling. We give him a napkin and he folds it into the shape of sadness. We ask after the photograph, but the man merely shrugs and fills his mouth with tapioca pudding. After a while, we begin to feel taken advantage of, but the man has already climbed into his beard and fallen asleep.

11. Thanksgiving

It is the first holiday since the fire, and I'm beginning to feel a hum that matches the resonant frequency of a rickety bridge. I try to keep my throbbing to a minimum. I go to the grocery store to buy everything we need for our pity party, leaving the ember at home. She would merely scoff at the sloe-backed journeyers trying to stave off existential dread with two-for-one cranberry sauce and made-from-scratch quinoa salad. After returning home, I gorge myself on proteins and water and RNA, a veritable panoply of life-giving consumerism. Unfortunately, I forget that embers hold only a nostalgia for that which has been consumed, so the perfectly done turkey is not as impressive as one burnt black on the heating coils of a 500° oven. The ember coughs a little and thanks me for all of my hard work, not uttering one sound of displeasure but communicating it clearly all the same.

12. Bob from Accounting

I fall into a rhythm at work. Every day, I'm given a new criteria to use when sorting the papers—by weight, by volume, by alphanumeric code, by histrionics, by daffodils—and I develop a new sub-criteria, a kind of coping mechanism. And each time I finish, the maybe-supervisor comes in and shoves all the papers into his briefcase. I consider just leaving the papers in their original piles to see if he'll notice, but the job is too important. It isn't just my soul to feed anymore. I have my eye on a new stack of kindling I've seen outside Home Depot last week. The ember has grown bored with my over-washed cardigans beginning to pill and *The Independent* delivered via wet sack to our front door. But all in all, the job is going well, and by well, I mean of course a soul-sucking vortex of drudgery creating a never-ending hole of existential despair. Not everything is sorting, though. Bob from Accounting stops by one rainy Thursday to make sure he has my address right. He could have just called or sent an e-mail or made his assistant Veronica send a howler monkey for confirmation, but he walked all the way up the nine floors to see me. That is my first clue. My second clue is when he very slowly, very sensuously honks my breast. I ask him how long he had been working on that Marx brothers impression. He hangs his head in shame and tells me about his plans for the weekend. He is going to nuke a microwave burrito until it falls apart and then watch back-to-back wood-carving expos. *Stop with these obscene euphemisms*, I say, *I prefer the groping*. So he places his hand back on my breast, the left one this time, as the right one gave him trouble before. There is nothing left to do but either sleep with him or toss his body out of a fifteen-story window, and since the office is only twelve floors, I follow him to a linen closet filled with monogrammed towels and washcloths. The sex is exactly like falling out a fifteen-story window. After we finish, I walk across the hallway to my office and Bob follows me. At first I think that he saw my pubic hair next to the monogrammed towels and felt a flare of matrimonial yearning, but it turns out that after the excitement of airing out his coccyx, he has forgotten my address again.

13. What Else is There to Do?

Three weeks after I started working the new job, the ember informs me that she is getting bored staying home all day. *So go for a walk.* I know that isn't what she's talking about, but I'm a little annoyed. Not only am I doing all of the work and paying all of the bills, but here I am, bringing home a nice meal of frozen fish sticks and moist towelettes and what do I get in return? I mean, I get that it is a lot to ask of the ember to avoid constantly setting the apartment ablaze in a glorious consumption of stone and flesh, but maybe it wouldn't kill her to wash a dish or two as well? The ember brings her flame to the very edge of diminishment. At first I think she's just being dramatic, but when I peer closer, I see the familiar goldish-brown spots of regret. *It's okay*, I tell the ember, *nobody's perfect.* Maybe she can come to work with me tomorrow? The ember grows even darker, and I understand it is not more of my presence she seeks. Maybe she could hang out in the vagrants' oil drum or start a couple forest fires? This brightens her up considerably, so I preheat the oven to 450° and try not to think about the smell of scorched flesh or the sounds my lover made when his lungs fused to bone.

14. I Take Another Lover

I sleep with Bob from Accounting twice, never knowing his last name or being able to say his first without a deep, racking cough. I've begun to feel a bit like an office cliché, so I decide it's time to find another lover. On my way home from work, I stop in the first bar I find with a name that isn't a pun. There are several older men clutching bottles of beer and a few lobbing darts at a bottomless pit. At first I'm disappointed this isn't a scene of youthful carnival, a dimly lit exhibit of greased-up bodies, but then I decide to dive fully into cliché. Perhaps I'll find a married man aching to slip on my skin like shaving lotion. But when I walk inside, the smoke turning my lungs into cardboard cutouts, the men glance up and then immediately return to their drinks. They are not interested in some silly girl trying to shake off her grief. Theirs is a need not of desire but of forgetting. Having a girl humid and breathless atop them would only recall the crocodile circling, the clock in its stomach ticking, ticking, ticking.

15. I Take Another Lover

I visit my dead lover's brother, hoping he will feel a physical obligation toward me that I can whip into a forgettable Wednesday tryst. I don't feel shame when meeting his wife or his five-year-old son, mostly because the little brat keeps calling me "Dear Liza," but I do feel an acute sense of foreboding when the brother invites me to dinner and loudly scrapes a lawn chair to the table. It is clear I don't belong, and yet I still show him my freckled arm and the soft white hairs of my upper lip. The wife piles roll after roll on my plate until there isn't room for any other emotion. I think it's a ploy to fill me with home until I hear the gurgling of her stomach after her second helping and understood how voracious she truly is. The brother invites me to stay for dessert, which appears to be a pile of rolls covered in cream frosting, but I decline. I wait in my car next to their house for fifteen minutes in case the brother changes his mind, but the lights in the house maintain the quiet glow of hearth and home.

16. I Take Another Lover

Finally, feeling the ache of unfulfilled spontaneity, I decide to find my ex-lover. I met him at a carnival that came one summer to the abandoned parking lot of the old mall. He was one of the teenagers running the Tilt-A-Whirl. For a bite of my cotton candy, he would give the ride a little extra tilt and a whole lot of whirl. We made out behind the Port-a-Potties, trying not to swoon under the fog of so many simple carbohydrates breaking down. I asked him what his hopes and dreams were, and he made a spinning motion with his finger. By that I understood he wanted me to lift up my shirt, but there were so many fathers walking around, I was afraid one of them might reach into my chest and steal my soul. So we both settled for mashing our eyeballs together while adults pretended not to notice. I'm not sure of his name or where he's from or even what he looks like anymore, so finding him might take some moxie. The old mall parking lot is mostly empty except for kids with fake graffiti t-shirts and fake graffiti skateboards and fake graffiti attitudes. I send up a smoke flare filled with throbbing reds and billowing yellows to remind him of the molded plastic backdrop of our tryst. One of the kids rolls by and yells *Merry Christmas, motherfucker,* which for them is pretty close to human speech. I consider stuffing the leftover flares down his pants and watching him erupt in a spectacle of light, but the other kids would probably make me their queen or something, and I don't need that kind of stress right now. I leave the remaining flares in the shape of an anatomically correct heart, hoping if my ex-lover stops by, he'll read between the lines.

17. And Then I Remember My Dead Lover's Face

Once there was a little girl who wanted to howl at the moon. Her father told her it couldn't be done. Her brother said, *get a life.* Her lover was the only one who believed. (He was not her lover yet but he would be soon.) He told her to shed her skin like a mountain and fur would grow in its place. He told her to bury her hands in the ocean and claws would emerge. He told her to swallow fistfuls of sand and her throat would be ready. The girl did everything the lover said, and soon she was muscled and panting. She ran the forest's path and bared her teeth at small, timid things. She drank from the river, snapping at leaves. She scratched her back on sharp rocks. She was covered in fleas, aching, hungered, with a singular purpose: to howl. She howled and howled and howled. But no matter her volume or timbre, the moon, a mansion of white, never moved, never bent, never broke. Her howl was not anger; her howl was not fête; her howl was a desperate chant: come down inside me and make me anew. Held tight to her passions, she ached to be free. When will I be who I am? She found her lover digging a hole and howled her remorse. The lover paused and considered her plight. *Do you want to return? Yes.* The lover grabbed bread and butter; he grabbed sugar cakes; he grabbed apples and sausage and cream. *Eat*, he commanded, *until you explode.*

She ate and ate, hoping to diminish her haunting. Finally, her stomach burst and she emerged, girl once again. No. Not girl. But what? She looked up at her lover (yes, now), who bared his teeth, sharp and silvered in the moonlight.

18. Worry is a Tooth Stained Red; Worry is a Sink Full of Dishes and a Dinner Grown Cold

I have spent too many nights in search of a face that was not my dead lover's and a body that was not a pile of ash, and the ember is concerned. The apartment has grown cold in my absence. It is December, and the ember does not know how to work the thermostat. Nobody on our street has put up any Christmas lights because most of the apartments are empty, so the only cheer to be found is in burning holes through my handful of books—Dickens, Tolstoy, Hemingway, Thoreau—none of which I've actually read. I kept hoping the words would slip from the pages at night and call to each other in my dreams. But I never once saw a Russian aristocrat or a cabin in the woods. Instead, most of my dreams are flashes of memory spun in a gyroscope faster and faster until they blur together—heat and light and sound—into a great wrenching cataclysm. And then my father appears and tells me what a disappointment I am. When I finally return from my last unsuccessful journey, the ember is waiting next to a pile of word-ash. She is quiet and ashamed, and I scoop her up into my bare palm, tiny mind-jolt of pain, and coo comforting words to her that evoke the memory of crashing trees. She falls asleep, or at least stops crackling, and I place her on the final uneaten page: the title page from *Nicholas Nickleby*. I promise her I'll try to do better.

19. It's a Secret

The customizable pet supply company is holding a massive Secret Santa. It doesn't just include the office workers but also management, middle management, custodial staff, secretaries, night watchmen, secret assassins, those heart-shaped bugs that hang out in the toilet stalls, and other building effluvia. Every single living or non-living entity is involved. Nancy, the self-appointed keeper of birthdays, carries around a giant red bag. I pull out a piece of paper folded into one of those middle school notes with a pull-me tab. Inside it is blank. Nancy winks at me and puts a finger to her lips. *Shhh*, she says, *it's a secret.* The rest of the afternoon is slated for business casual puppeteering. Since the only thing I have at my disposal is stacks and stacks of paper, various office supplies, and Nancy's occasional hovering grin, I staple the sheets of paper into the shape of an office building. I populate the office building with tiny paper people and tiny paper desks and tiny paper chairs and tiny paper houseflies, including the one that's been dive-bombing my head all morning. I cut out windows so the tiny paper people can look up at the blue sky, but then I realize it's raining and the tiny paper people are afraid. I close the window and pull down the shades for extra measure, but now the tiny paper people are becoming depressed. They shuffle from their tiny paper desks to the tiny paper office fridge and back. They begin to slump in their tiny paper chairs, even though I made sure they were ergonomic for maximum paper efficiency. Several tiny paper people begin coughing into their hands—a bug is going around the tiny paper office. They are no longer crisp white but a dull, listless gray. One tiny paper person opens a tiny paper envelope and discovers that his wife's cancer treatments, the ones in the tiny paper hospital down the street, are hundreds of thousands of dollars and their tiny paper insurance company has denied their claim. He grabs a pair of tiny paper scissors, puts them to his throat, and threatens to do himself in. The rest of the tiny paper people watch, their tiny paper bodies shadows of the beautiful white cut-outs they were just moments ago. Before the tiny paper person can commit tiny paper suicide, I grab the building and drop it off at Nancy's desk with a note that reads: *To Santa.* It's her problem now.

20. The Reason for the Season

Having learned my lesson from Thanksgiving, I ask the ember what she would like for Christmas. She huffs and puffs before identifying a large plastic Christmas tree covered in dazzling lights that she can chew and chew and never devour. This is entirely doable, but I also want more than just the typical sparkle: I want a few surprises to unfurl like quicksand. I spend the entire afternoon at the thrift store buying old wicker ornaments and tacky-bright garland and popcorn to make into strings and even a couple glass bulbs (vulgar portends) and lights like tiny barrels ready to rat-a-tat-tat color across the apartment. All of these I carry home and place one-by-one on the plastic Christmas tree. The ember has spent the day finding bell ringers hunkered outside shopping malls and stinging their bell-ringing hands again and again and again and again and again and again and again—all to test their faith on this the holiest of days. She comes home in a peculiar mood, dismayed, no doubt, at how little adversity the bell ringers could take, and perhaps even a little nervous at how hostility becomes an itch that never stops blossoming. When she arrives in the living room, however, all is forgotten, all is mind-blank joy at the humming, sprawling light-orgy in front of her. She flits from one plastic bloom to the next, each light-point tripping the walls fantastic. She flames as large as I've ever seen her. She chews on the plastic for a while, and then, not quite sated (as I predicted), she moves on, still-hovering, tentative, to a piece of unsalted popcorn. This she explodes in a sizzle-crunch of flame. *Careful, you don't want to burn the house down.* Tiny nugget of yearning, she pops off one piece of popcorn after another, the blackened string drifting to the ground. *Okay*, I say, *okay now.* She moves on to the wicker ornaments, crumpling the intricate patterns into memory. All the while she grows larger and larger, from apple core to cantaloupe to great, yawning abyss. She winds around the tree, growing in both size and voltage, and with each breathe-heave, a glass bulb shatters and her flame crackles and this rich and ruby-throated song rises into carol, into hymn. The plastic tree, the one she was supposed to chew and chew and never devour, has begun its own unfurling—the plastic drooping into acid-colored puddles; the smoke, once barely flicker, now green-black and heaven-bound. I'm trying not to panic, to choke on the images of my father, brother, lover, all torn from my thoughts and shoved, limb-splayed and skin-shattered, into the space behind my eyes (flecked now with my father's phlegm-colored work boots, my brother's irregular mole, my lover's patch of hair from his navel to his dick).

I take one last look around the burned-out apartment, turning this, too, into memory, and then I am gone.

21. The Patch of Grass on Which I Wait Grows Cold, Then Damp

As the ember devours the apartment and everything inside, I watch from several blocks away, waiting for the sound of fire trucks, waiting to see if she'll make it out before the final tamping. The fire trucks come, and the other apartments (empty, blessed holiday gift) shiver next to such wreckage. They are untouched beyond the smoke slipping through the duct work to emerge with each new occupant's first bated breath on the eve of move-in day. Then the new occupants will call their fathers, panicked at the smell (feeling somehow that it is their fault), and the fathers will drive the three or four or five hours to the apartment, the one they checked so thoroughly, testing all of the light switches and pushing at questionable-looking bulges in the drywall and running all the faucets simultaneously, and during the three or four or five hour drive, they will become angry, then livid, then ravenous at those fat, greasy slumlords who trap their daughters in asbestos-filmed fire pits. Those men, those greedy, lying, unconscionable men will pay. Oh yes, the fathers growl, clutching their steering wheels, imagining the flutter of throat-bones between their hands, they will pay. Hours pass. I wait for the ember to return. The fire trucks leave and the police leave. Nobody comes. All is quiet night-bloom of stars, bright and steady, in the cold and empty air.

22. How to Mourn What is Lost in the Fire When What is Lost is the Fire

First, lay your body against the damp-chilled grass. Take one staggered breath, the air knifing down your throat, and then another. Lay very still and wait for the blood moving behind your face to stop. Wish for a brandy or a scotch-whiskey or even a very high-proof beer (several, actually). Wish for a very large knife from your kitchen so you can slice down your chest and stomach and create a haven for some small, half-blind creature stumbling around in the dark. Yearn to make an even larger, more important sacrifice of your body. Remember more important people that you've lost and understand that they have all returned to star-glimmer and do not miss you. Contemplate a greater wreckage of your body, until the roiling ugly mass inside you can be seen. Sit up. Feel the dampness on your neck and shoulders and back through your sweater, an ultra-thin $25.99 from Target that will dissolve by the third wash. Wonder why a clothing company would make such a stupidly thin sweater, and then wonder why you would be dumb enough to buy it. Wonder what other idiotic things have rent your body. Remember the ember's very simple request and how you had to fuck it up. Stand. Walk for a while through neighborhoods you've never seen. Stare too long at the soft, asthmatic whine of streetlamps. Do not contemplate what secrets lay beyond the checkered curtains of darkened houses. Walk until you no longer feel the crunch of gravel and dirt underneath your feet. Keep walking. Imagine that when the sun rises, you will have travelled through your grief and into a meadow, wind-whispered and grass-eternal, a place so beautiful and new, it rips you open by its presence. Imagine what this would feel like. Hold on to that feeling, a tiny flame inside your chest. Nurse the flame with bits of blackened lung and half-eaten bread until it pops, a sound like forgiveness.

23. We're Sorry to Inform You

The flame inside your chest is not the ember. The ember is not inside of you or outside of you. You cannot fix your mistakes so easily.

24. Stirring Dull Roots

The next day is sky-smeared and opaque, so I hardly notice when the sun rises. It doesn't matter. I've fallen asleep underneath an oak tree that keeps waking me with its treacherous whispers. It wonders if I'm taking up too much space in the world. Perhaps I would be happier if I slipped quietly back into nightmare. The tree shivers with mirth at my croaking. I finally stand, my body a hollowed-out skin-tomb, and begin walking. The words the oak whispers are a promise: a ship slipping into the darkness. The pull is moon-strong, and the oak has a deep, husky voice like someone I can trust. Best to keep moving.

25. Metaphors

I walk through centuries of trimmed hedges and lights in the shape of reindeer. Ahead of me is a field and beyond the field is a forest and beyond the forest is __________. The field is winter-bleak; walking across it is a constant erasure. Perhaps it once held tall grasses. Perhaps birds once called across the great expanse and exploded into morning. Perhaps it once was a song. It's difficult to see to the other side, to lilacs and hyacinth pushing their way into the sun-shy world. Cruelty and memory are always lapping at each other's heels like a dumb dog wagging its tail into a necrotic stub. The forest is not the same one I travelled to with the ember, but all forests are simply a continuation of that great practical joke. My feet splinter grass-nubs filmed with frost. There is not enough sun and not enough heat yet to melt them. I think about a picnic, but I don't have a blanket or a noose or Tupperware filled with regret. I should probably eat something, but the emptiness inside of me has other ideas. The emptiness is an indie rock song with two acoustic guitars and a cello and no vocals. Once I cross the field, there is only the forest. I am not nervous, not exactly, but the dead trees are such an obvious metaphor that I wish the ember were here to set the entire place ablaze. Since she is no longer my past perfect tense, I wait for the trees to grow faces and begin to scream.

26. Inside the Forest

The forest is suspiciously quiet when I enter. The trees are not whispering dirty limericks or flipping me off. It begins to snow, just like a screensaver. Up ahead is a small shack. There is no smoke coming from the chimney but the whole building is covered in a gray-green film like a smudged painting. Inside is a small stove along with wooden spoons and pots and pans hanging from nails. The pots don't hold my memories and the pans are not warm with expectation. Everything is just what it is: cold to the touch, signaling nothing. I fill a pot with water and chop up some onions and carrots and garlic sitting on the counter. I don't remember them being there a moment ago, nor do I remember this whole plucked chicken. I toss it in as well, lighting the base with a match from a matchbook suddenly in my pocket, which is very strange since my jeans don't technically have pockets but those sewed-in suggestions of pockets (pocket-shade, pocket-memory). The fire is small and ordinary—no chance of my heart-flame underneath. I allow the vegetables and chicken to simmer and then spoon some of the mixture into a wooden bowl. The first sip tastes just like the chicken soup my father made when everyone in the house was sick with measles.

27. The Ghosts Emerge

They appear one-by-one: vestigial synapse-hum, more corporeal than I expected. First my brother: meaty and grimacing. He wants to know if his *Maxims* made it out okay. I shrug, and he tells me to stop being such a cunt. Next my father: his favorite plaid shirt, washed and ironed by my mother into hearsay. *I have some three-alarm heartburn,* he guffaws. *I have some feetburn and neckburn and skinburn. Wish someone would come and put it out!* Finally, my lover. His face like rusted iron giving way, like a sunrise through a cloud of bees. Eyes and lips and hair, all normal. And yet. And yet? He walks over and tries to touch my face but cannot—his hands are merely a suggestion, a Manager's oversight. *Why are you being so difficult?* There are tears at the corner of my eyes but they haven't been approved yet. *The important thing to remember*, he says, *is that we are all in charge of our own destinies. We get what we deserve in the end. Well*, I say, *which is it?* They all smile and nod. Then he and my father and my brother swirl into the soup I have not touched since their arrival. I pour it back into the pot for some other widow to drown in.

28. Then & Now

Outside the shack, the world has shifted. Before, the trees were evergreens. Now, they are evergreen+. Before, it was winter. Now, it is winter+. Everything is just a little bit brighter, a little bit deeper, all of it underlined with a thick red pen. My teeth, moss-covered, grim, search for radio signals. I wonder if I go inside the shack and re-emerge, if everything will be again as it was, or if it will be even more. The trees are breathing loudly—they are asthmatic in their insistence. To my left is a tuft of grass like any other but a bit more edged. I touch the very tip of the tallest blade and it pricks my finger, drawing a tiny blood-bead, round and thrumming with secrets. The pain is so small and so sudden, it is almost a joy, a child's balloon floating toward the sky. I put my finger in my mouth and there, in the space where my finger once was, the grass has shifted just to the right, barely an afterthought. If I can place my finger, now blood-free, into the sliver of space that remains—it is not land or air or sky but gathered darkness, cloaked in existence. I put both hands in and pull and pull until it is big enough. I only pause a moment before reaching my body inside.

II. The Flame

1. After the Fire (Redux)

Through earth-pull and heart-seed and genderless slipping, I arrive: the last loose tooth of Little Mavis' worry-stained gums. I am not fire nor heat (not yet), but only a brief mind-clench of pain in the final tendon connecting her upper left molar. I am buffeted by fingers and star-lobbed wishes and each crimson breath, but still I hold fast. No amount of tangoing will rent me from this place. I know she is not the one I am seeking, the one whose hole I could never solder shut, yet she holds a hint of the other: the little bit of crust at the corner of her eyes, the untenable collection of DNA that could have formed a monkey or a dogwood or a Boston Crème Pie but didn't, the fart that makes a sound like eeeeEEEEE, the quiet space inside her she thinks is her soul, which also makes a sound like eeeeEEEEE. Here in this fortified nook, I take stock of all I've consumed: blood and bone and loose, soggy flesh and wood and concrete and paper and nylon and plastic but not her. Not her. It is all one long mouse-breath anyway, and by that I mean a striving toward that first, best void, when everything was a dream of particles colliding, before we exploded all over the furniture and made a real mess of things. I only have two, maybe three days as the ache in Mavis' left upper molar before she worms me out of her mouth and out of her life. Then I'll move on. I have no need to explore a world without love and heat and passive aggressive e-mails. Better to flame out in one last wrenching and leave Carl and Judy to mop up after me.

2. A Very Brief Trip

I underestimated my autonomy; my get-up-and-go surrendered to the firing squad. I only make it as far as a brief bout of indigestion in the stomach of Boots, the family cat. This is quite embarrassing, or it would be if I had the capacity for masochism and self-doubt. Boots has very little duplicity and almost no tendency to self-sabotage. If I can't watch her return again and again to the muscled pit of her undoing and know, deep in the throes of my chemical reaction, that my presence is but a salve and my absence will hasten her unraveling, what's the point? Here, in the stomach roiling with off-brand cat food is emotion rising and falling and rising again, like a seasick humidor. There is no anxious narcissism to fuel my longing, no quiet nights when that old tinny lockbox begins to howl and she gives me the soft skin of her palm even though she knows it will hurt (because she knows it will hurt). Here there is only each hour passing unseen into the next, and from the moment I sprang from her fingers—a chemical burn of rage and panic and love, a deep, knotted thought brought suddenly to term—I knew that would never be enough.

3. Corporeal Form

It is time to burst into blossom; it is time to finally combust. I consider the fireplace pilot light, that quivering, cupped offering, but I know it is too much, too soon. Such sudden optimism would leave me heady and stumbling; I would consume all in one ruinous breath. No, better stick to something with edges, some shallow piece of marginalia. I choose instead the upstairs sex candle (Yankee Candle, pumpkin pie scent). In this January gloaming, it is finally lit. Carl and Judy are doing their own version of combustion: Carl, from behind, thinking of the small-breasted, big-lipped girl at the Honda service kiosk who always pronounces his name MISter Franklin. As he grips the fleshy tomb of his wife's stomach, he imagines the girl's voice grown deep and evergreen, speaking of rivers and rocks and one naked leg beckoning, and the water, yes, oh, the water, pulling him deeper and deeper and ohgodyes deeper. Judy, her fists filled with cloth, thinks of a cottage on the shore of some distant lake with baby blue walls and soft wicker chairs and the sound of the waves, gently lapping, steady and empty and waiting for her, no husband no father no curious mailman, just her and no one else, lapping, lapping, and then, yes, and then, she closes the door and she is sweetly, blissfully, finally alone.

4. Memory & Desire

Before I can be snuffed out in a ponderous sigh, I take flight, this time to the gas stovetop where Judy has begun cooking black bean soup. The soup is a protest, one full of artifice. Her soul is a staged photograph of brie. In another time, another place, she would vibrate: thinner, happier, healthier, and always in better lighting. She has made a resolution to Be Happy and Be Her Best Self and Follow Her Heart, though the starting gate is rusted shut and the forecast says it's monsoon season. For now, she can live within the blurred edges of sepia. For now, she can eat only when spoken to. Carl grunts at the bowl of black bean soup and low-fat cheese quesadillas. *Needs a protein. Needs some meat.* Judy's soul needs some protein; she is dangerously close to falling out of her three-story balcony and into the rosebushes. If called by any other name, he would still be an ass. She won't utter the sound of the last doctor's visit; she won't be seen whimpering. *Shut up*, she says, *and eat your damn soup.*

5. The Pilot Light

Her sound is a whisper across oceans and time: *come, my breathless, my beloved, come.* They can't hear it in their concrete boxes, but I can. *Come, my wounded, my sun-sodden lover, come.* It is a high, still ache through the trees. It is the blue that is black that is night. *Come, my first grafting, come, my straight shooter. Come.* Each call is a ratchet that will never stop turning: *come, come, come, come.* In dawn-stream, in daydream, in silver-moon gleaming, she calls: *hush, sweet little teeth-clench, and follow my sound. I won't give you heartache or last weekend's lies; I promise you headswell; I promise you filling; I promise to keep coming and coming until you say stop. But will you say stop, clever goose-downy pimple? Or will you remain, pliant and trembling? Your word, one reply, is all that I need. Say yes.*

6. Carl Gets Cold

I tried not to swell; I tried to stay clean. I let her sound echo all through my last trembling, but still her voice beckoned and still she remained. And then, it was snowing. And then, it was star-shine. And then it was aching in Judy's brie-covered soul. It was only a whisper; it was only a moment. Carl bent down and fumbled the ball. In those last shaky heart-breaths, he wished for some pie.

And then.

And then.

It wasn't my fault.

7. Filled to the Brim; Brimming to Bursting

Oh when the saints come marching ooooh sweet child of mine I bless the rains down in Africa gonna take some time but don't you forget about me don't oh oh oh for the glory of England oh for the glory I know-oh-oh, oh for the glory of En-gland strumming on the ole' banjo singing boom shakalaka shakalaka shaka-HEY let's hear it for the boy let's give the boy a hand nah nah oh yeah once I was a poor boy nobody loved me and you were a poor girl from a poor family but don't worry oh yeah 'cause I'll be there you're all I ever need I'll be there so take oooon me take on me take meeeee on and I'm hungry like the wolf so fix it dear Henry dear Henry dear Henry fix it ah yes push it mmmmmm push it real good B-I-N-G-O oh B-I-N-G-O and shishka was his name-oh. OI!

8. There Were No Survivors, Not Even the Cat

There once was a structure with beating hearts inside, and now there isn't. Nothing to scream and scream and scream about. The last few sun-dips are mere memory and those memories are locked in a pile of wood-ash. Once-Carl clicked the pilot light, the flammable goose. It wasn't my choice after that. Moving on to the next threshed-open shore, the next cavernous horizon. There are so many places that can hold me but so few that won't disappear with the next light. And then there's the matter of matter, which I require from time to time. My needs are few; my desires vast. How long before I can nestle in the soft skin of her palm once again, feel her heartbeat ticking through her veins? Even a damp washcloth is preferable to this. Such ruin, such famine, such wide-open longing, and then a house comes down around me. What is it that you meat-lockers do? Make lists? Put one foot in front of the horse and cart? Rip your body open in one long heart-scream?

9. Into the Woods (Again)

The forest is closed today. The forest has lost its sense of humor. Twelve feet of snow: a thick accumulation of uncertainty. *Come back next Tuesday*, the trees say. *Don't let the door hit you on the way out*, the robins chirp. *A penny saved is another penny*, one confused naked mole rat mumbles before digging his own grave. I don't need an invitation, just a couple of loose atoms and boom, here I am. Sometime today the snow will become rain and gather into a suffocating blanket. *Be wary—you are especially susceptible to winter's deceit*, the trees warn. But then again, when was the last time the trees were on my side? I bounce from laden pine needle to laden pine needle, each one sighing at my arrival and not-so-subtly checking the time. The snow shifts closer to ruin, and I know they will blame me when every last creature drowns. So off I go, not to grandmother's house, but to another factory of maternal willingness, the zoo.

10. The Monkeys are my Favorite Exhibit

The black jaguar, which was nobody's favorite animal but the oldest one at the zoo, has died. It was a vague reminder of the darkness that will one day consume us all as it paced back and forth and back and forth and back and forth behind the iron fence. Nobody really liked watching it, but it was a kind of obligation toward our younger, more vulnerable selves. Not everything can be monkeys dangling from ropes and throwing feces. Not everything can be a big black bear scratching itself against a rock. Sometimes you have to take in a breath and hold it as long as you can. Sometimes you have to weep openly at the terror of unyielding credit card applications in the mail. There is no part of your body that you love.

11. My Pet Iguana Once Gave Me Salmonella

Past iron bars holding nothing, I arrive as the tepid bulb inside the salamander terrarium. Nobody cares much for the salamander; everyone wants to see the tarantula or the kingsnake. Marisol, one of the volunteers, checks her phone again. It is a Tuesday morning and there are no buses full of children crawling through her daydreams yet. One day Marisol will become a veterinary technician. Right now she waxes poetic about bite strength and keeps the lamps lit. The public water fountain tastes like regret: a slight copper aftertaste and a warmth spreading through your midsection as your mistakes slip one by one into your bloodstream. She touches the oil of her forehead and smears it across one of the cardboard displays: a snake unhinging its jaw and eating a terrified rabbit whole. Each winter is an exercise in mnemonic devices: Please Excuse My Knotted Noose; This Isn't the Life that I Wanted. Check the food, check the water, check the temperatures, check yo'self before you wreck yo'self. Her boyfriend was her imaginary friend growing up; now he Snapchats pictures of his pecs and does another ten reps at the gym. She wants things to get serious; he wants another bowl of pasta. Maybe she could nudge him toward something more analog. Before I go, I burst the bulb to give her something sharp to hold on to, before she disappears in one long hiss.

12. $85 a Year; Make Checks Payable to Judy Franklin, Treasurer

My next stop, a bright yellow sign (one of three) outside a neighborhood: HOA dues now due. The redundancy makes me itchy. Across scaly lawns are castoff newspapers in plastic sleeves, the brightness a sign of the times: orange, yellowish, nearly clear. A few have shed their skins: juiced, then reformed. Mealy word-shod silt. Black boxes stand sentinel; flags up or down, it doesn't matter. A woman walks two Pomeranians. She imagines a Pit Bull charging at her precious fur babies and then she imagines blowing it away with a shotgun. She imagines blowing away the Pit Bull and the Doberman and the Rottweiler and then she imagines blowing away Teresa, the snide little receptionist at her doctor's office who makes snide little comments about this being her third appointment that month. It's not her fault she has a weak immune system and dirty little children with their dirty little hands touch everything. Dogs are so much cleaner. So much more like people. She would imagine blowing away the children, but she knows that is a bridge too far. Two doors down, a boy dribbles a basketball in the street. The net is a whispered conversation among lovers, the last donut in the break room. Soon, it will fall. The tonk-tonk-tonk of the basketball can be heard in five darkened bedrooms. The boy thinks of nothing but layups and jump shots and the rhythm of his sole. Inside the house, there is a threat of rain. Outside, all is rainbow. The woman walking the dogs crosses the street when she sees him. She's not racist, per say, she's just careful. Here, everything is layered, but all the layers are skin. There is nothing with wings, nothing I can sink my teeth into.

13. I Find a Friend

On my way out of the neighborhood, I run straight into a horsefly. It seems too cold for horseflies, but what do I know? I'm merely ongoing combustion. The horsefly is big and its eyes are multifaceted and it shivers a little when it sees me. Maybe I remind it of its horsefly mother and horsefly father who succumbed to a child's magnifying glass when the horsefly was three days old. I flame low so as not to attract too much ire. After all, loose and untethered like this, we are reviled. The horsefly spins in a little circle, which I take to mean hello. Then he zigs up and zags left, which I take to mean how do you do. I am charmed by his antics, which seem entirely without sleaze. I pick up a tree splinter and turn it to ash. The trees whisper to themselves, *I knew it, I knew it!* The horsefly nods at my offer and we fly away before the trees get any bright ideas.

14. BFFs on the Prowl

The horsefly takes me to his favorite garbage bin outside La Tolteca Mexican Restaurant. Everything is fried and refried, and I worry about his cholesterol. He has how many days left, and he's going to spend them shoving his silvered eyes into discount meat? I try to convince him that the dumpster outside of the Market Bistro is better, or at least fresher according to the dead dog on Silverado Avenue, but he throws his body against the metal wall again and again and again. I get the feeling he is no longer enthralled by my presence, so I give him some space and find a child's onesie to curl into. It has a bitter tang, like all once-loved things, so I find a pile of Styrofoam take-out boxes instead. The sound of my consumption is like a man getting run over by a waterfall, so I stop and simply rest on the pavement while the horsefly eats. *Come get me when you're done*, I say, though I'm not sure he hears me.

15. Was It Something I Said?

When I wake on the oily pavement, the horsefly is gone. My flame is as low as I can remember it; I need something throaty and quick. Nearby is a church full of mourners who ready their ruby-throated songs. But that's a bender, and I just need a hit. I find a boy with plastic army men covered in slime. The boy cannot remember his father who left when the boy was still a brief conversation in a Red Lobster bathroom. The mother has not set foot in a Red Lobster since. The boy covers each soldier in Nickelodeon Gak and then draws two expert lines underneath his eyes, imagining himself a four-star general weeks away from retirement. He reaches for the cat, Henry Whiskerton III, who darts away before this man-child can declare war. For Henry Whiskerton III, all movement is intention; all consciousness is combat. I slide, hallowed and hungry, into the first. The slime quakes and expands and explodes with a pop. The boy throws the soldier into his neighbor's back yard. The plastic is slower, a full breath in and then out, as my flame grows heaving and red. I must be careful not to feast on dry ground. The rain has stopped and the grass is open season. There are many more soldiers along the path and only one soft-headed child, but I demure. One is enough for today.

16. Return of the Prodigal

I'm thinking about heading up through the sky until I reach the sun. It is not mother or father to me, despite what people think. It is all-consuming light born of darkness, like Uncle Charlie who wasn't allowed around little Marie after that one incident on the Fourth of July. It is a kind of resignation, hurtling oneself into the sun, and one I don't make without first checking the time. But there doesn't seem much else to do except flicker high and flicker low and one day flicker out. Once I've made up my chemicals, I turn around and there he is: the horsefly. Back like he never left me lonely and wandering. He buzzes a trepidatious circle around me, which is not an apology so much as a warning not to question his fortitude again. I agree, and we are happy as hooligans, chortling around the campfire. Since the horsefly has just fed on necrotic horsemeat, it is my turn to pick our destination. I choose the abandoned storefront on Route 13, just before the Auto Zone. Inside are ants, termites, a couple smaller flies, a raccoon, and a plastic baby doll with slow-moving eyes. None of the other residents are particularly fond our arrival, and though I want to tear this motha down, they don't seem apt to raising the roof. So we simply mill about, pushing our faces through stifling air and sawdust. The horsefly thinks this is all kind of lame and I agree, so we leave the bugs to traipse up and down the wooden beams and the raccoon to do unspeakable things to the plastic doll.

17. Burn

The horsefly and I hover over two children playing in a sandbox. The girl is making an amorphous blob that she will name Steve. The boy is watching the girl with a face like falling rocks. Both have kicked sand beyond the breaking point and have zero regrets. Once the blob has risen into a slightly larger blob, the boy stomps it back into no-shape. The girl looks at the blob and looks at the boy and looks at the blob and punches the boy in the nose. It is not even hard enough to bend, let alone break, but still the boy wails. The horsefly, having seen a thousand small boys cry a thousand sad songs, plummets and attaches to his neck. *Ow*, the boy says. The horsefly is intransigent; the boy is inept. *Ow! Ow!* The boy is all hollow sound; each cry echoes through my chambers. *Please*, the boy says. My insides are my outsides, yet I still feel a stirring. The horsefly returns, limping with girth. *Oh*, I say, *you're a girl.* She bats her blood-soaked eyelashes and grins. *Enough to go around.* This wasn't the original plan; this wasn't my direction. But inside the boy is a nugget of meanness, and I want to know how it tastes. We both find a patch of nubby pink skin and dig.

18. The Next Backyard

The boy's fear had a fresh briny taste, and I forgot how bulging and furrowed such focus could make me. I wanted layers, but a long, thin hum might suffice. Afterwards, we no longer zig and zag; we choose the shortest distance between two smorgasbords. The next is a woman asleep in a hammock. I choose the papery skin of her wrist while the horsefly, like a bull in Madison Square Garden, goes right for the neck. *Oh God*, the woman cries. It is a sound like a door being ripped off its hinges. Her panic is lemony tart, a lifting of the lips into oblivion. I try to hold on, but her feet are not pudgy or small; they deliver her quickly to salvation. She shakes us like room keys, and though there are many more oceans to plunder, we sigh at this lost cause. *Next time*, the horsefly says, *no escape*.

19. The Amazing Race

In the crepuscular dawn, one hundred men and women toe the line, ready their flimsy bodies to soar. Here the foundation is steady; there is nothing to shake us. The first is a gathering of meat and muscle all working toward the same goal. We descend and immediately are swatted away. We descend again, this time from an unseen spot, and are swatted again. Through the rhythmic breath-stomp of progress, the man can hear our descent; he knows the fruits of our labor. The next is a boy who flails at our first traipsing. His arms are a windmill and his hands bust up our expectations. There is nothing for us here; the blood is stretched safely beneath Lycra. Besides, the emotional whirlpool I so desperately crave is nothing more than a tickle of annoyance and a brief bout of indigestion. Even if I could unzip myself past their defenses, it would land me in a tepid mud puddle, not a monsoon.

20. Merryview Hospital: The Nursery

The horsefly has an idea; she leads us to the first moment of swelling. Inside the pre-sealed doors, past the scrubbed clean smell of rotting, we arrive: all are bound and tooth-gapped; all are somnambulant. *Ready?* We burrow ourselves in gluttony, and then the true opera begins. One little heart-swell of panic; two little heart-swells of panic; three; four; five. Each flame-stroke is disaster; each heart-cry is pure. I am lifting, I am spinning, I am jellin'. I've got a lovely bunch of coconuts, deedleedee. *Calm yourself,* the horsefly says, but I am no longer here, please leave a message with the receptionist on Wednesday. Oh when the saints come marching in. The room is a shimmer; the room holds a monster; the room is quaking and light. The horsefly is insouciant, though her wings are tornado. Why bury us both? Here is my final groundswell; here is my brief adieu: the blankets have gone up in flames. Soon I will be past the breakers. Soon my light will go out. Ashes, ashes, we all fall down.

21. The Sprinklers Turn On

The song stops; the music dies. I can't remember what I had for dinner last night. Was it nighttime, or was it the slow unfurling of tomorrow? Each point of light explodes but not inside me. The sound of the ocean is disaster. There were others, but I can't see them. Each gathered fist washes clean from me. I can't remember her name.

The girl.

The girl with fire in her eyes.

The girl who burned her father, brother, lover.

Where are you?

III. Interlude: The Ghosts Speak

1. The Brother

the world is an oyster but you can't   force it past the
teeth   dad calls them skidmarks   nothing to be
ashamed of   just needs a little fortitude   hear
that?   laundry's not going to do itself   last
night, beyond the x-ed out channels   the x-ed out
eyes   I saw the universe   a bonafide nip slip
gray and swimming through the snow   why can't
he just pay a little extra   it's not like we're poor or
something   get out of my room get   dad says
its natural   inside, it's poison/outside, it dries up like
dead fish   dad says   he says the lake is filling
up   the lake is full of birds   they don't drown
they   don't   they are arrows   they circle
and circle and they find   it's okay   dad says,
waterfall   dad says, cross currents   dad says,
go to sleep   I know you hear the trees outside my
window   branches, branches, branches

2. The Father

Q: How much does a fat ghost weigh?
A:

Q: What is the sound of one ghost hand clapping?
A:

Q: When is the best time to see a ghost?
A:

Q: What did the ghost say to the little girl who burned
his house down?
A:

Q: How many times a day does the ghost circle the
house?
A:

Q: When does the ghost start to plot his revenge?
A:

Q: Should the little girl be afraid?
A:

Q: Should she?
A:

3. The Lover

this house is too goddamn small (feel this electric current moving inside me); it's thursday, did you let the technician in (my throat is working and working); goddamn it, the kitchen is a mess (open your hands and let me crawl inside); just once i'd like you to think before you open your mouth (bloom, thistle, and open wide); why do you always have a goddamn headache (my breath blossoms inside you); you know i have to work late (another memory aches this night); what did you make for dinner (each hour is a promise ticking closer); it better not have any fucking kale in it (hush, darling, and close your eyes); i'm going out don't wait up (burrow deep and find where i'm hidden); it can't be broken again what the hell did you do (each tick of the clock brings me closer to you); why don't you try fixing it for once (a ravaging thought emerges this night); you know i don't like that ipa shit (the flush of your skin in my hands); goddamn it not another girls night (let us quiet and join); why are you always going out (i want to hear your pleasure); sharon's a fucking bitch you know i'm right (why not); wait where are you going (please); you're coming back right (please); you aren't leaving for good (goddamn it); wait just wait (i said please); i'm sorry okay i'm sorry (bitch).

IV. Reunion

1. Upon Waking as a Cloud: The Flame

I thought my time had blown dry; I thought I was up a tree without a hunch. But last night was a journey I had to take. Through gorging and fullness, through smoke and flame, through the last little tickle of solace, I snuffed out, then emerged: gathered mist overhead, ready to spill. No longer combustion but a different process altogether: the expectation of dry land, desire quenched. Now loose and free-floating; now tepid and swollen: my many hearts are unchanging. I will find her.

2. Upon Waking as a Ghost: The Girl

Once I slipped through the no-space, the slit at the center of the universe, I tumbled, broken-bodied and aching, into lost time. Not no-time, but minutes and seconds and hours gathered like a pile of moth-eaten blankets at the back of grandmother's closet: folded, then forgotten. What use would she have for such dead weight? Once, she wrestled over meaningless numbers, but now who gives a shit? Let the money burn, her savings leak out from heating bills and grandchildren's birthdays and made-up traumas by her less-than-perfect nieces. With him, she kept a tight grip on everything; without him, she relaxes into paralysis. Tomorrow, she will eat cold soup. Next week, she will shut up half the house. Next month, who knows? The time I now inhabit is folded and re-folded and re-re-folded until it is a loose confederation of moments sloughed off the rest of the world: a sneeze held in during a tense board meeting; the cry of a morning dove that no one heard; a half-eaten Panini run over by a truck; the last three voicemails left by an anxious husband for a wife killed by a drunk driver; a puddle of rain under the awning of an abandoned storefront. I slip into each moment, inexplicable witness, and watch until the memory fades and the next wrinkle emerges.

3. The Reality of Water: The Flame

My first day is spent over a dry river basin. It fills me with dread and an ache just above my right filament, but this isn't why I'm here. I must keep moving; each drift may bring me closer to her. The horsefly would say that the opposite might also be true: I may never fully bridge my expectations. But the horsefly is gone; she will never be my comrade in terror again. Earlier, a seagull hovered near my sodden stratus. I thought she might tramp the sky-mall with me, maybe even journey to the center of my dreams, but instead she hung me out to dry. Soon I grow thin; the ache is now inflamed. Like a discordant tune, I head in the direction of water. A little damp earth is all I need. Instead I find feast: a flooded plain. I gather each morsel, a slippery sin, until I risk falling. Once sated, I know what I feared: I traded one set of teeth for another. This hunger, too, will leash me—each day a series of trades, each havoc wreaked from the inside out. Move forward and hope for the mist.

4. Out of Time: The Girl

The last moment of countenance is the one that freed me: a three-digit locker combination suddenly recalled by a once-girl in a dream. It was November and the leaves were on fire. She was naked, no, she was wearing a sombrero, no, she was ten feet tall and her crush, David Davidson, thought she was a freak. Then she was in school and the bell was an avalanche and she couldn't remember the combination to her locker, inside of which was the name of every My Little Pony. And then, suddenly, there it was, numbers buzzing overhead like a sign: 5-7-5. It is a terrible combination, she thinks as she wakes, a 36-year-old woman with two kids and a mortgage and a husband she no longer loves. She closes her eyes, ready to return to a world of minor anxieties. I slip from her dream into the bed beside her. Her forehead is damp, so I reach forward to brush her hair. My hand passes straight through her.

5. The Great Escape: The Flame

The lesson was vast: don't succumb to one last boon. Don't put one foot before the weather. And yet, here I am, above seaweed and sea-salt and small skittering creatures. But this time it's different, I swear. I'm reaching and reaching and not finding purchase. Instead, my swelling leads me in a new direction: down. Down, down. From gathered smoke to twenty-five droplets to a vast open sea: each transformation wrecks me all over again. In this sudden volume, I lose myself. The harder I focus, the more I dissolve. Perhaps I need a new life vest, a motto emblazoned in the sea. Relax. Chill out. Go with the flow. It's working—my mood is thawing: I see the arc of possibilities. I can tickle the tide fantastic at Adak, I can slip into something more comfortable at Nemuro, I can cocoon in my new favorite bay. What's your pleasure? I hear China is nice this time of year.

hey

hey

hey you

6. Home: The Girl

Something feels different, though I can't place my finger on what. I also can't place my finger on who, or where, or when, though 'placing' is just as problematic as 'finger.' The more time I spend in this shape, the less I maintain it. I seem to be slipping into fumes. No longer in the bedroom of the once-girl, I exhale through her chimney and out into the sky. Is this what it's like to be flame? I was never one to seek danger or thrills, so this vision is a little beyond me. I seek solace; I seek gravity. I wonder if I can find my old apartment, the one that suffered two catastrophes. But the hour grows stale, and I can't remember the shape of the place, let alone such onerous things as numbers. In fact, my whole foundation of language seems to be loose. If I don't concentrate, words jiggle and float before my eyes. Hot dog. Ellipses. Rutabaga. Soundproof. Beige. Okay. Shelve each errant sign and tamp down the excess meter. Nothing like a little weightlessness to throw everything off balance. Worse is I can't shake the feeling that there is something, someone, near. Reaching out. About to take hold. Okay, breathe. I can't remember the apartment, but there is another place I do. It is a cavern of ashes, a museum of rot. Still I glide, brash, funnel-like, toward home.

hey

hey

wait

i know you

7. Inside the Sea: The Flame

I once sought turbulence, the varied emotions within. Now, pot-bellied, cosmic, I'm ballooning with life, each meanderer clogging my ducts, threatening my reflux. I felt an oil rig, reticent earth-carver, break open inside me. No one cleaned up their mess. And still the ocean croons: Pollock and flounder and stingray and dolphin and coral and sea whip and sole. Major tides, minor tragedies—they're all the same: awash in a literal sea, all is muted and primed. I dive (without ambulation—all is inside me) to my glorious depths to see what the fuss is about. At the edge of darkness, I see them: a panoply of rhythm, a calliope of color. Is this for me? Dozens of creatures, their hearts slippery when wet, sway to my tides. Clownfish tango in anemone. Jellyfish light this motha' up. Hydromedusas shake what their mommas gave them. Stingrays waltz in ¾ time. Nudibranches mambo down the line. And a single lionfish, gaudy, grand, raises the roof. I watch for an hour or maybe a year (time is a fool's game, unwelcome advice) and then, to show my delight, I clap a wave of small creatures their way. *Dinner is served.* Before I can witness the massacre, I surface and wait for the silent sun. Perhaps, once it sets, I'll feel different. Perhaps, moon-washed, somnambulant, I'll get pulled in another direction.

8. Surrounded: The Girl

each morning i rise and reach for the glass that is no longer there and I remember again what you did like we were worse than some dumb fag putting his hands where they didn't belong so don't give me that innocent act every damn one of you has something you're desperate to hide

(help)

listen babe we need to talk and not a word not a whisper not a whimper from you until i'm done so your little pyro stunt was cute and all but the big boys have some corporeality to work out and since it's you who got us here in the first place and since I can reach out and touch you now what are you going to do about it

9. The Pull: The Flame

The time of transformation has come: the moon is full and luminous. All around I can feel the loosing of minds, men on the brink of reality. The tap-tap-tap of a nail against porcelain at the Lighthouse diner. The moment before he grabs the waitress by the throat. The decision whether or not to squeeze. Thirty old men and women at the Alzheimer's unit, swimming through heart-song, suddenly rent. Waking in a space that is bad, bad, bad, get away, now. Hands reaching, hands holding, strong hands, bad, bad. *Oh Henry, why are you letting them hurt me? Henry, they're hurting me, please.* And a nurse with the bad, bad hands trying to be gentle but firm. *Gladys, it's me. Time for bed, Gladys.* And a girl, not yet twenty, walking the path to the graveyard, the lights from the campus behind her. Don't let them see me, she thinks, though she doesn't know why. Don't let them come. All of these voices, sonorous, tidal, in and out and in. But there is one, quieter, stronger, a taut thread aquiver. It is meant for me, though I can't hear its voice. It is whisper-thin, diluted, desperate. I still my restless waters and listen.

10. The Girl

(please)

11. The Final Journey: The Flame

It only takes a century (collapsed in a moment) to find the source of her calling: the house where I first emerged. Sparked into life, cocooned in so much rubble and flesh, the source of my hunger. It was the girl who gave me solace, gave me home. She is the one calling across time and space. She is the one whose spark grows dimmer. Slick, rubber-banded, I hop from sea to estuary, tributary, river, pond, wetland, puddle—whatever will hold me. I try to waft, I try to take flight, but now, gravity-bound, I can't loosen up. I am a feeble banding of molecules, yet deeper, within each electrical flash in the pan, rests every quailing that headed my way. Before, each emotional guzzle was fodder for the flame: here, then gone. Now, the temperaments linger; I can't seem to shake them. I am sodden, I am weighted, I can never break free. Soon, on the back of Tramp, the neighbor's black lab who ran through a sprinkler, I see my life's work. Still wreckage, the once-house with once-people. Inside, or rather, beyond, is the girl: haunted. It is a puzzle for the ages: not quite water, not yet mist—how to reach her?

12. Silenced: The Girl

Listen, do you hear us // taking out the trash // we won't be ignored // the leaking dishwasher // your time for speaking is done // the water spots on the glasses // no more of your stupid whore lies // the burned-out light bulbs // who did you open your legs for // the empty ice-cube tray that no one remembered to fill // how many men // the broken back step // how many women // the leaf inexplicably in my bed // do you know that you're dirty // my mother's gold wedding ring // do you know you're unclean // the dusty blinds // you leave us no choice // the family photos leading up the staircase // this is for the best // the broom in the hall closet // you have to understand // my mother's jewelry box // we all have a part to play // my brother's stack of *Maxim* magazines // we all have certain expectations // the chipped clay pot from middle school used to collect coins // certain obligations // the alarm clock // even if you want something more // the blue and yellow and pink sheets from each bed // you have to know your place // what was on the sheets from each bed // be a good girl, now // the answering machine asking you to leave a message after the—

13. Rescue: The Flame

Hung out to dry, or rather, shaken loose from the back of Tramp, I am temporary, floating, when I see her light go out. Time slows and I arc, headed again toward the mundane: my extinction. Why not reach into every last wish that pummeled me and turn them toward some greater good? What do I have to lose?

One final breath. And

WhyCan'tHeDoTheDishesForOnceINeverToldHerI LoveWhereIsMyFavoritePleaseOhGodPleaseWhen WillItBeMyTimeMyDon'tTellASoulOrHe'llPleaseIf YouGiveMeThisIPromiseI'llDon'tLeaveMeGiveUpWhy Can'tHeJustWhereAreMyOhGodNotAgainIfOnlyShe'll NoticeAndThat'sNotEvenCountingWhenWillItHappen AndWillItOhGodPleaseJustListen—

I pack each wish tighter until they center inside, mouse-breath, plosive. Then, ready for nothing, I release.

14: Breathe: The Girl

Holy shit, it's you

15. Moving Forward: The Girl

I don't want to talk about it. The past is an 8-bit recording of my ancestor's first root canal. Nothing to see here. This pile of rubble, this collection of broken-down things, why did I let it haunt me? No matter. Shake it off. Here is a partial list of things I haven't lost: a feeling of weightlessness, a too-thin sweater from Target, Pizza Hut's Cheesy Bites pizza, toe lint, a general belief in the good of humanity, Puffs plus lotion, an ineptitude for Jeopardy, an atavistic fear of thunder, frizzy hair, corporality, a loathing for stepping in wet spots while wearing socks, lust, my soul. What was lost: my ability to give a fuck. Part animal, part sky, I zoom past mailboxes and rotting decks and a feral cat giving birth beneath my neighbor's porch, past the trees that have nothing more to say, then stop, circle back. Even with all this buoyancy, I am not without weight. I can't leave without her.

16. Reunion: Girl & Flame

Girl

Bag of blood and bone
again, I bare my teeth
and let my hair down.
I'm less fretful than
before—more feral,
more cavernous. There
is so much room inside
me.

Be seen and not heard;
shrink to fit the space
you deserve. Fuck that.

It is time to emerge; it is
time to take flight.

But first I reach out my
hand—

Flame

I hear her call: no
longer a whisper among
thieves. It is single,
profound, a break-in at
dawn, a noose she has
loosened and burned.

The way back dims.
How can I find her,
Polaris, among the riff-
raff, inconsequential
shimmer and gloam?

Inside me, something is
catching

Heave, vibrato my lover
awaits

—uncurl the fist—

—and I'm no longer
alone.

Burn, as hard and fast as
you can.

There is space for you
here in my ribcage—
this final soldering, this
timid beating.

Don't turn back. This
blooming is shadow, not
wound.

And us?

Just one more turn
of the screw.

I found you.

What about you?

Here, in these shallow
bones? Here, in this ark
barreling through the
sky?

Quick, the light: the last
birds call their undoing.

Gray skies open;
headlights rusted shut.
Onward, upward,
through.

Acknowledgements

An excerpt of this novella was chosen as a finalist for the *Iron Horse* Photo Finish Contest and was published in *Iron Horse Literary Review* in January, 2016.

Selected excerpts have also been published at *The Conium Review Online Compendium*.

About the Author

Melissa Reddish's short story collection, *My Father is an Angry Storm Cloud*, was published by Tailwinds Press in 2015. Her flash fiction chapbook, *The Distance Between Us*, was published by Red Bird Chapbooks in 2013. Her work has appeared in *decomP*, *Prick of the Spindle*, and *Northwind*, among others. Melissa teaches English and directs the Honors Program at Wor-Wic Community College.

When not teaching or writing, Melissa does stereotypical Eastern Shore things, like eating seafood smothered in Old Bay and playing fetch with her black Lab.

Melissa's black Lab is named Blue.

Blue is a good dog.